Ducks Disappearing

Phyllis Reynolds Naylor
pictures by Tony Maddox

Atheneum Books for Young Readers

While Father was at a meeting, Willie and his mother had lunch in the motel.

"Look at the ducks!" Willie said as he ate his soup.

A mama duck and her ducklings were marching proudly across the courtyard.

"Let's count them," said Mother.

"One, two, three, four, five, six . . . seven, eight, nine," said Willie.

A duckling ran out of the bushes.

"Ten," Willie added.

Another duckling came out from around a lamppost.

"Eleven," said Willie.

One big duck and eleven ducklings.

"We will be staying at this motel," Mother told the waitress. "I'd like to see if our room is ready."

"Go ahead," said the waitress. "I'll watch Willie."

Willie stayed at the table eating his soup. He counted the ducklings again. Then he blinked.

This time there were only *ten*. One mama duck and ten ducklings.

He went out into the courtyard. When the big duck saw him coming, she waddled away, her ducklings behind her. Willie counted once more. Only ten ducklings.

He looked in the bushes. He looked behind the lampposts, but he could not find the other duckling. He remembered when his goldfish back home in the pond were disappearing one by one; a raccoon had been eating them.

He went back inside.

"Excuse me," he said to the waitress. "Did you know there are ducks in your courtyard?"

"Yes, someone saw them at breakfast," the waitress told him. "One mother duck and eleven ducklings."

"Well, now there are only ten," said Willie.

"I'm sure the other one is out there somewhere," the waitress said. "There's no way it could leave the courtyard. How about finishing your soup?"

But Willie didn't care about soup. He went back outside and counted again. "One, two, three, four, five, six, seven, eight, nine . . ." Now there were only *nine* ducklings. He looked in the bushes, behind the lampposts, and under the benches. Then he went inside and up to the desk in the lobby.

Mother was talking to a woman in a gray jacket with her name on the pocket.

"Excuse me," Willie said to the woman in the gray jacket. "I saw a duck with eleven ducklings in the courtyard, and now there are only nine."

"Those are wild ducks," said the woman. "They don't belong to us."

"Our room will be ready soon, Willie," said his mother. "I'm getting the key."

But Willie didn't care about the room. He went back to the courtyard. The mama duck was pecking for bugs in the grass. Willie counted her ducklings. This time there were only *seven*.

He looked everywhere—in the bushes, behind the lampposts, under the benches, among the rocks. Seven ducklings. That was all. Something bad was happening to the ducklings, and it was happening very fast.

He went inside and over to the bellman who carried suitcases.

"Excuse me," he said, "but ducks are disappearing! There was a mama duck and eleven ducklings in the courtyard, and now there are only seven!"

"Maybe they flew away," said the bellman.

"They're too young to fly," Willie told him. "They're so small I could hold one in my hand."

"Beats me!" said the bellman.

Willie was worried. The next time he counted the ducklings, there were only five.

He ran inside and over to a man who was vacuuming the carpet.

"Excuse me," he cried, "but something is happening to the ducks in the courtyard! Just a while ago there was a mama duck and eleven ducklings, and now there are only five."

"Well, they're not in my vacuum cleaner," the man said with a laugh, and went on with his work.

When Willie went outside and checked again, there were only three ducklings. He was very upset.

The mama duck was upset as well. She was quacking loudly and walking around in circles. The three ducklings were following behind her, walking in circles too. And then, as Willie watched, *whoosh!* One of the ducklings disappeared!

Willie leaned over. There was a storm drain in the grass, with a big metal lid on top. The holes in the lid were too small for the mama duck to fall through, but large enough for her ducklings.

Willie got down on his hands and knees. There were ten ducklings at the bottom of the storm drain, cheeping loudly.

Ten? He counted again. Ten ducklings down in the hole and two on the grass made *twelve* ducklings. One duckling must have been in the storm drain a very long time.

Willie threw back his head and yelled as loudly as he could, "Help! Stop what you're doing and help these ducks!"

A man who was cleaning the swimming pool hurried over.
The waitress came out, as well as the bellman, the man who
was vacuuming the carpet, and the woman in the gray jacket
with her name on the pocket. Willie's mother came too.

Everyone looked down into the storm drain where Willie
was pointing.

"Those ducks don't belong to us," said the woman in the gray jacket.

"They're wild ducks. They don't even belong in the zoo," said the man who had been cleaning the pool.

"They don't even belong to the state," said the waitress. "I think they came down from Michigan."

"Well, *I* think they belong to all of us!" said Willie.

Everyone looked at Willie.

"Let's lift the cover off," said the bellman to the man who had been vacuuming the carpet.

"I'll get my leaf net," said the man who had been cleaning the swimming pool.

Soon the mama duck and twelve yellow ducklings were marching proudly around the courtyard once again. And the woman in the gray jacket with her name on the pocket said that she and the others would look after the ducklings, and would cover the storm drain until they were old enough to fly away.

"Good!" said Willie, and went back to finish his soup.

For Sophia and her first word
— P. R. N.

Atheneum Books for Young Readers
An imprint of Simon & Schuster Children's Publishing Division
1230 Avenue of the Americas
New York, New York 10020

Book design by Becky Terhune

The text of this book is set in Berkeley.
The illustrations are rendered in watercolors.

First Edition

Printed in the United States of America
10 9 8 7 6 5 4 3 2 1

Library of Congress Cataloging-in-Publication Data
Naylor, Phyllis Reynolds.
Ducks disappearing / by Phyllis Reynolds Naylor ; illustrated by Tony Maddox.—1st ed.
p.   cm.
Summary: Willie solves the mystery of the disappearing ducklings and involves the motel
staff in the rescue operation by telling them that the ducks belong to everyone.
ISBN 0-689-31902-9
[1. Ducks—Fiction. 2. Hotels, motels, etc.—Fiction. 3. Lost and found possessions—Fiction.]
I. Maddox, Tony, ill. II. Title.
PZ7.N24Du   1997
[E]—dc20
95-10281